GW00854829

Will it be a nig.
Christmas's grandson

Dyan Sheldon is a children's writer, adult novelist, humorist and cat-lover. Her children's titles include *A Witch Got on at Paddington Station*, *The Whales' Song* and, for Walker Books, *Sky Watching*, *Harry and Chicken*, *Harry the Explorer* and *Harry's Holiday*, as well as the picture books *I Forgot* and *Love, Your Bear Pete*.

Robert Crowther is the creator and illustrator of a number of highly successful novelty books, including *The Most Amazing Hide-and-Seek Alphabet*, *Pop Goes the Weasel!*, *Robert Crowther's Pop-up Machines*, *All the Fun of the Fair*, *Robert Crowther's Pop-up Animal Alphabet*, *Animal Snap!*, *Animal Rap!* and four Lift-the-Flap Books for young children. He lives in Oxfordshire.

Some other titles

The Baked Bean Kids
by Ann Pilling / Derek Matthews

Beware Olga!
by Gillian Cross / Arthur Robins

The Finger-eater
by Dick King-Smith / Arthur Robins

The Haunting of Pip Parker
by Anne Fine / Emma Chichester Clark

Little Luis and the Bad Bandit
by Ann Jungman / Russell Ayto

Sky Watching
by Dyan Sheldon / Graham Percy

The Snow Maze
by Jan Mark / Jan Ormerod

The Unknown Planet
by Jean Ure / Chris Winn

DYAN SHELDON

A NIGHT TO REMEMBER

Illustrations by Robert Crowther

WALKER BOOKS
LONDON

For Judy
D.S.

First published 1993 by
Walker Books Ltd, 87 Vauxhall Walk
London SE11 5HJ

This edition published 1994

2 4 6 8 10 9 7 5 3 1

Text © 1993 Dyan Sheldon
Illustrations © 1993 Robert Crowther

Printed in England

British Library Cataloguing in Publication Data
A catalogue record for this book is available from the British Library.

ISBN 0-7445-3197-7

CONTENTS

CHAPTER ONE

It was Christmas Eve. The night
was crisp and cold, and the stars
shone like fairy lights in a dark and
cloudless sky. Father Christmas
whistled as he marched out to
the stable.

A small, thin figure stumbled
behind him. This was Father
Christmas's grandson, Sam.
Sam was having trouble walking
because his boots were too big.

At the entrance to the barn, Father Christmas stopped. "Ho-ho-ho!" he said, gazing up at the glittering sky. He looked back at the stumbling figure.

You know, Sam, this is going to be a night to remember.

Sam was digging snow from his boots.

Father Christmas frowned. Sam was a very modern boy. He was so modern that he wasn't really interested in filling stockings or in driving through the night in a sleigh pulled by eight reindeer. He was interested in television and videos. He was interested in loud music.

Stop dawdling! This is the greatest night of your life.

Sam fell over in the snow. "I'm too young for this, Grandad!" he said.

"Too young? Nonsense. I was your age when I first went out. I couldn't wait to see the sights. The pine trees of Toronto! The chimney-pots of London! The candles of Düsseldorf!"

Sam groaned. "But I don't care about the chimney-pots of London, Grandad. I'd rather see a film."

Father Christmas blew his nose. He had a bit of a cold himself. "What nonsense," he said.

Sam bumped into him with a cry of surprise. Sam was not only having trouble walking; he was having trouble seeing because his hat kept sliding over his eyes.

Sam tripped into the barn.

He collided with a wall.

17

Sam staggered after him. "It's not that, Grandad – " He bumped into a post. "I just don't think I'm cut out for this job. I've never really seen myself as a delivery boy…"

Father Christmas
spun round. He
looked closely at
his grandson. It
was true. He didn't
look right. Perhaps
Sam was going to
be an even bigger
disappointment than
Father Christmas had feared.

"Delivery boy!" spluttered Father
Christmas. "What do you mean,
'delivery boy'?" He pointed at the
sleigh. "Father Christmas is not a
delivery boy! He's jolly old St Nick
and he brings happiness to millions
of children all over the world!"

"I was hoping for a bit more fun," said Sam.

"And who said it isn't fun?" thundered Father Christmas.

"You did," said Sam. "You said you wanted a helper because you were bored with climbing over rooftops on your own. You said you were tired of lugging that heavy sack all by yourself."

Father Christmas straightened his hat. It was true, he *had* said that. He *was* a little bored with climbing over rooftops on his own. He *was* tired of lugging that heavy sack all by himself. Father Christmas frowned. He was sure that being St Nick used to be fun. He just couldn't seem to remember when.

"Never mind," said Father Christmas gruffly. "Fun isn't what matters. What matters is that there was nothing else I ever wanted to do."

"Well, I rather fancy being an astronaut," said Sam.

Father Christmas turned on his heel. "I'll get the deer," he said.

CHAPTER TWO

Together, Father Christmas and Sam
harnessed the team.

"Not like that!" shouted Father
Christmas. He wrenched the straps
from his grandson's hands. "Can't you
see you're making them nervous?"

Sam glanced over his shoulder. "They're making *me* nervous, Grandad," said Sam. "They look like hat racks and they smell like old socks."

The reindeer's ears went up.

"Humph," said Father Christmas.
Sam tried to help him load the sack
onto the sleigh.

"Is that the way I showed you?"
Father Christmas roared. He tugged
the bag from Sam's grasp.

Sam collapsed with a groan. "No wonder you're always complaining about your back. That thing weighs a ton."

Father Christmas and Sam took their places in the sleigh.

"Stop fidgeting!" ordered Father Christmas, giving his grandson a shove. "Why can't you sit still?"

"Because this seat's so hard and uncomfortable," said Sam. "Couldn't we at least get some cushions?"

The reindeer pawed the ground.

"This sleigh is like something out of the Stone Age," said Sam.

"Humph," said Father Christmas. "Let's go."

Together, Father Christmas and Sam began their journey round the world.

CHAPTER THREE

Father Christmas wouldn't let Sam
drive. "You'll hit something," he
said. "You'll go too fast. You'll crash."

Father Christmas wouldn't let Sam carry the sack.

Father Christmas wouldn't let Sam fill the stockings.

Sam was chased
up a tree in
Toronto.

He got stuck
in a chimney in
London.

He was almost
set on fire in
Düsseldorf.

31

"You see!" fumed Father Christmas as they veered sharply towards the rooftops of Amsterdam. "You're completely useless."

Sam held on to his seat. "I'm not useless," he protested. "You're the one who won't let me do anything."

"Do anything?" repeated Father Christmas. "What can *you* do besides turn on a television set?"

Sam held on tighter as the sleigh pitched and bucked. "I didn't *ask* to come," he managed to gasp. "I wish I'd stayed at home."

They skidded to a stop. Sam fell out of the sleigh.

"No!" raged Father Christmas. "I'm the one who wishes you'd stayed at home. This is the worst Christmas Eve I've ever known."

CHAPTER FOUR

Sam pulled himself back into his seat. He pushed his hat out of his eyes and shook the snow out of his hair. He looked around. "Uh, Grandad," said Sam. "Grandad, don't you think this roof is a little icy?"

"Icy?" shouted Father Christmas. "Of course it's icy! It's winter, isn't it?" He hurled himself from the sleigh.

Sam looked for something to hold on to. "And steep," he added. "Icy and steep." He peered over the side. "And you've parked on a slope."

"Please be careful, Grandad!" called Sam.

"I think Comet would make a better jolly old St Nick than you. That's what I think!" Father Christmas roared.

And then he fell off the roof in a shower of gifts.

CHAPTER FIVE

Sam brought the sleigh down to the
ground. The reindeer watched as he
helped his grandfather to his feet.

42

Sam took off his hat and stuck it behind his grandfather's back. "If only we had some cushions…"

Father Christmas collapsed with a sigh. "Cushions are the least of our problems," he groaned. "Not only is this the worst Christmas Eve of my life, but it's going to be the worst Christmas Eve for a lot of children, too." He waved towards the presents scattered over the street.

The reindeer looked over their shoulders.

Sam looked at his grandfather.

Father Christmas looked at his sack, still caught in a tree. He shook his head sadly. "For the first time in hundreds of years, jolly old St Nick won't complete his rounds."

Sam cleared his throat. "Well …
I suppose *I* could always deliver the
rest of the toys," he said softly.

"You?" asked Father Christmas.
"You, Sam Claus, act as delivery
boy? I thought you weren't cut out
for this job."

The reindeer shuffled restlessly. They jingled their bells. They glared at Father Christmas.

Father Christmas glared back at the deer. "Oh, go ahead," he groaned. "I'm in too much pain to argue with any of you."

"Well, you were right about one thing," said Sam, tossing the suit into the back of the sleigh. "This is going to be a night to remember all right."

CHAPTER SIX

Contrary to what Father Christmas had feared, Sam didn't drop the sack, or break any presents, or mix up the toys. But he did sing as he filled the stockings. The reindeer tapped their feet and shook their bells.

Father Christmas lay back
listening to the music in the air.

Suddenly Father Christmas saw
himself as a boy. He was lying on
his bed, reading a book about
sailing ships. He heard his father
yelling at him for wasting his time.

50

Sam sprang from the chimney in a spray of snowdust. "You know, this isn't so bad after all," he called.

Fun!
Father
Christmas
watched
Sam spin
before the
stars. He
saw himself
as a boy,
laughing and
leaping down chimneys. He saw
himself scattering presents and
racing through the night. He heard
his father complaining that he did
everything wrong. He heard himself
shouting that he wished he'd stayed
at home.

Sam climbed into the driver's seat and tugged at the reins. "You know," he laughed, "I think this is even better than being an astronaut."

Father Christmas leaned forward.
"Did I ever tell you that there was a
time when I thought I wanted to be
a sailor?" he asked. It was something
he'd forgotten himself.

CHAPTER SEVEN

Also contrary to what Father
Christmas had feared, Sam didn't
cause a crash. But he drove so fast
that the wind whistled past them
and the rooftops blurred.

The reindeer leapt over clouds
and galloped through moonbeams.
Sleigh-bells and laughter echoed
through the night.

For the first time in months,
Father Christmas wasn't tired. His
bones didn't ache and his feet didn't
hurt and he wasn't feeling the cold.

Sam looked down at the world shining below them. "There really are some great sights, aren't there," he said. He laughed as he guided the team round a tower.

"Ho-ho-ho!" Sam roared.

"Ho-ho-ho!" roared his grandad.

The reindeer snorted, their bells rang out, and the sleigh sped across the moon.

"Merry Christmas, Sam!" laughed Father Christmas.

"Merry Christmas, Grandad!" laughed Sam.

MORE WALKER PAPERBACKS
For You to Enjoy